Children love a secret of any kind, and secret places have a special fascination for them. Written over fifty years ago, The Secret Garden *is a story whose freshness and charm continues to appeal to generation after generation of children.*

THE SECRET GARDEN

Frances Hodgson Burnett

retold in simple language
by Joyce Faraday
with illustrations by Joy Shufflebotham

Ladybird Books Loughborough

The Secret Garden

Mary Lennox was a spoilt, rude and bad-tempered child. She was never really well, and she was thin and miserable, with a sour face. No one liked her at all.

None of this was really Mary's own fault. She was born in India, where her father worked. He was always busy with his work, and paid no attention to his daughter. Her mother was very pretty, and cared only for parties and pleasure. She left Mary in the care of an Indian nursemaid, who gave the little girl everything she wanted so that she would not cry and upset her mother. So, not surprisingly, Mary grew up into a spoilt and most unpleasant girl.

One hot morning, when Mary was nine years old, she had a strange feeling that something was wrong. She stayed in her room and heard shouts and cries and the patter of hurrying feet, but no one came to her. She lay on her bed and fell asleep.

When she awoke, the house was silent. Still no one came to her, and she was angry that she had been forgotten. Suddenly, the door opened, and two Englishmen came in.

'Why was I forgotten?' Mary said, stamping her foot. 'Why does nobody come?'

'Poor little kid!' said one of the men. 'There's nobody *left* to come.'

That was how Mary learned that her father and mother were dead. They had been killed by the disease sweeping the country. Most of the servants had died too, and the rest had run away. Mary was quite alone. There was no one left in India to look after her, so she was sent to England to live with her uncle, Mr Craven, at Misselthwaite Manor in Yorkshire.

In London, Mary was met by Mrs Medlock, her uncle's house-keeper. Mary disliked her at once. But then, Mary disliked everyone. Mrs Medlock thought Mary was a plain, rude child — and she was quite right. As they travelled north she told Mary about the house. It sounded very grand and gloomy, and stood on the edge of a moor.

'There'll be nothing for you to do, and your uncle won't bother with you,' said Mrs Medlock. 'He's got a crooked back. He was a sour young man until he married. His wife was a very pretty girl and he worshipped her. When she died, it made him queerer than ever. He's away most of the time, so you'll have to look after yourself.'

It was dark when they got out of the train. A carriage pulled by two horses took them to the house, but Mary could see nothing outside in the rainy blackness.

'What's the moor like?' she asked.

'It's just miles and miles of wild land,' Mrs Medlock replied. 'Nothing grows there but gorse and heather, and nothing lives on it but wild ponies and sheep.'

At last, the carriage stopped in a courtyard. A huge oak door was opened by a butler. 'You're to take her to her room,' he said to Mrs Medlock. 'The master is going to London tomorrow and he doesn't want to see her.'

Mary followed Mrs Medlock upstairs and through many corridors to a room with a fire burning and supper on the table.

'This is where you'll live,' Mrs Medlock told Mary. 'Just see you stay here and don't go poking round the rest of the house.' This was Mary's welcome to Misselthwaite Manor. It made her feel cross and unwanted and lonely.

The next morning, Mary awakened to find a housemaid lighting her fire. She was called Martha and she smiled and chatted as she worked.

Mary was not used to friendly servants. In India, she had never said 'Please' or 'Thank you', and once she had even slapped her nurse's face when she was angry. Somehow she knew that she must not treat Martha this way. At first, Mary had no interest in Martha's chatter but, little by little, she began to listen to the friendly Yorkshire voice.

'Eh! You should see all my brothers and sisters in our little cottage on the moor,' Martha said. 'There's twelve of us and my father only gets sixteen shillings a week. My mother has a job to feed 'em all for that. The fresh air on th' moor makes 'em strong and healthy. Our Dickon, he's twelve, he's always out on th' moor. He's good wi' animals. He's tamed a wild pony.'

When Martha had to go away, Mary went out to play.

'Go and look at the gardens,' Martha had said. 'There's not much growing now, but it's lovely in summer!' She had stopped for a second and then said softly, 'One garden has been shut up for ten years since Mrs Craven died. Mr Craven locked the door and buried the key. He hates that garden.'

The grounds of Misselthwaite Manor were huge. They were divided by high walls so that there were many gardens. In some, there were flowers and trees and fountains. In others, vegetables were growing. Doors led from one garden to the next, and every garden looked bare and wintry.

Presently, an old man came through one of the green doors. He looked as bad-tempered as Mary herself.

'Can I go through that door?' asked Mary.

'If tha likes,' he replied. 'There's nowt to see.'

Mary was hoping to find the door to the locked garden. She tried many doors but they all opened easily. There was one wall covered with ivy that seemed to have no door at all. She could see trees behind the wall. A robin on a high branch burst into song. She stopped to listen, and the cheerful notes brought a little smile to her unhappy face. She wandered back to the old man. He ignored her and went on digging.

At last she said, 'There's a garden over there without a door.'

'What garden?' he asked gruffly.

'On the other side of that wall,' she replied. 'I heard a robin in the trees there.'

13

The old man stood up and a smile spread across his face. Mary saw how much nicer he looked when he smiled. He whistled very softly. Over the wall flew the robin and landed by the man's foot.

'Here he is,' he said quietly. 'He always comes when I whistle. Isn't he a grand little chap? Look, he knows we're talking about him.' The robin, plump and scarlet-breasted, hopped about pecking at the earth. Ben Weatherstaff, the gardener, went on digging. 'He's the only friend I've got,' he said. 'When he's not with me, I'm lonely.'

'I'm lonely too,' said Mary. 'I've never had any friends.'

Ben stopped and looked at her. 'I reckon we're a good bit alike,' he said. 'We're not good-looking and we're as sour as we look.'

Mary had never thought before about her sour face and her bad temper. Now that she did, it made her feel uncomfortable. Just then, the robin flew up into a tree and sang with all his voice.

'He's taken a fancy to thee,' said Ben. 'He wants to be your friend.'

Mary looked up at the robin. 'Would you be my friend?' she asked. She spoke softly and kindly, instead of in her usual hard little voice.

'Why,' said Ben, 'tha said that like a real child instead of a sharp old woman. It was nearly like Dickon when he talks to th' wild things on th' moor.'

The robin flew over the wall.

'There must be a door to that garden,' Mary said.

'Well, there's none to be found now,' snapped Ben. 'Don't you go poking your nose in places where you don't belong.' And he walked off without saying goodbye.

Mary spent most days out of doors. She ran to keep warm and the cold wind brought a pink glow to her cheeks. Each night she felt hungry and ate a good meal. After supper, she liked to sit by the fire and talk to Martha.

'Why does Mr Craven hate the locked garden?' Mary asked one evening.

'It was Mrs Craven's garden. She loved it,' Martha said. 'She was sitting on the branch of a tree when it broke and she fell. She was hurt so bad, she died. That's why he hates it. He won't let anyone talk about it.'

Mary had never felt sorry for anyone before but now she understood how unhappy Mr Craven must be. The wind blew across the moor and moaned and roared round the house. Martha called it 'wutherin'. Mary listened to it and through the 'wutherin' she thought she heard a child crying.

'No,' Martha answered when Mary asked. 'It's only th' wind or the scullery maid. She's been crying all day with toothache.' And Martha left the room hurriedly.

The next day the rain poured down.

'On a day like this at home,' said Martha, 'we all try to keep out of each other's way. Except Dickon. He goes out in all weathers. He brought home a fox-cub that he found half drowned. He's got a crow too, called Soot.'

Left on her own, Mary decided to explore
the house. She followed corridors and went up
and down stairs. In the stillness, she heard
again the faint sound of a child crying.

As she stooped to listen at a door, another
door opened and out came Mrs Medlock.
'What are you doing here?' she demanded.
'Get back to your room at once!'

Mary was angry. She knew she had heard the cry and she was determined to find out what it was.

The rain storms passed. 'You wait until the sun shines on th' golden gorse and th' heather,' said Martha.

'I'd like to see your cottage on the moor, and your mother,' said Mary.

'Tha would love my mother,' Martha answered. 'She's kind and hard-working. When it's my day out and I can go home to see her, I just jump for joy.'

'I'd like to see Dickon too,' said Mary.

'Yes, you'd like him,' Martha said. 'Everyone likes Dickon.'

'No one likes me,' said Mary sadly.

'Well, maybe that's because you don't like other people,' Martha smiled.

'I never thought of that,' Mary replied.

Mary found Ben digging in the garden.

'Spring's coming,' he said. 'Th' plants are workin' under th' soil. You'll soon see crocuses and daffydowndillys.'

The robin flew over. When Mary followed him to his perch on the ivy-covered wall, he hopped down onto the soil. Mary crept nearer and he twittered as though he was talking to her. Now she was very close to him and she felt so happy she scarcely dared to breathe. The robin pecked in the earth for a worm, and suddenly, in the soil, Mary saw a rusty key!

'Perhaps it's the key to the Secret Garden!' she thought. She slipped the key into her pocket and ran indoors.

After supper, Martha told her about her day at home. 'Mother says you must be lonely here,' said Martha. 'She sent you a present to cheer you up.' She brought out a skipping rope with striped handles and showed Mary how to skip with it.

'Your mother is very kind,' said Mary, wondering how Martha's mother could have spared the money to buy her a rope. Now, wherever she went, Mary skipped, and the more she skipped the stronger she grew.

One morning, the robin was watching her
from his perch on the wall. Suddenly,
something happened that felt like magic! A
gust of wind blew the ivy on the wall and,
under the leaves, Mary saw a door! She felt
for the key in her pocket and tried it in the
lock. It was very stiff but she could just turn
it. The next second, she was in the Secret
Garden! Her heart thumped as she looked
round. It was over-grown and untidy, but she
thought it was the loveliest place. She saw
green shoots of bulbs pushing up through the
soil, and pulled the weeds away from them to

make way for the crocuses and snowdrops. She went on weeding and clearing dead leaves and grass. Time slipped by.

At supper-time, she longed to share her secret with Martha but she dared not in case she should be forbidden to go again to her Secret Garden. Instead, she said, 'I wish I had a bit of garden to grow things in.'

'That's a lovely idea,' Martha answered. 'I'll get Dickon to bring some garden tools and some seeds to plant.'

Mary worked in her Secret Garden every day. Everything was starting to grow. Mary was careful that Ben Weatherstaff never saw where she went. One day, he said to her, 'This fresh air is doin' thee good. Tha's fatter and not so yeller. Tha looked like a young plucked crow when tha first came.'

Mary laughed. She liked Ben now, even on his grumpy days.

One day, she saw a boy sitting under a tree. Two rabbits and a pheasant were near him, and a squirrel clung to the tree above his head. They were listening to the tune he played on a pipe. He got up slowly so as not to frighten the animals. His blue eyes smiled from his round, rosy face. 'I'm Dickon,' he said. 'I've brought tha garden tools and some flower seeds.'

His smile was so gentle and kind that Mary forgot to be shy. She felt that if animals trusted him, she could trust him too. After a while she asked, 'Do you know about the Secret Garden?'

'I've heard of it,' he said, 'but I don't know where it is.'

Making sure no one was watching, Mary led him through the door in the wall. Dickon was amazed. He looked round at all the plants and trees. 'All these will grow,' he said. 'There'll be flowers and roses everywhere. In a few weeks, the leaves will be sprouting.'

They worked together, weeding and pruning. Mary felt she had never known anyone like Dickon. Trying to speak in a warm, Yorkshire voice like Dickon's and Martha's, she asked, 'Does tha like me?'

'Eh!' he laughed, 'that I does, an' so does the robin.'

After dinner, Mrs Medlock came to take Mary to see Mr Craven. 'He's going away tomorrow and he wants to see you first,' she said.

Mary felt a little afraid and very awkward and stiff. But Mr Craven wasn't a bit frightening, nor was his back really twisted. His face was handsome but looked full of worry and misery. He asked if there was anything she would like. Mary asked for a piece of garden to grow her own flowers.

'Of course,' said her uncle. 'Take any bit that's not being used.' Mary knew which bit this would be. She could call the Secret Garden her own!

In the night, Mary was awakened by heavy rain and the wutherin' of the wind. She felt angry that bad weather would keep her indoors. She couldn't sleep. As she lay tossing in bed, she heard the crying again. 'That's never the wind,' she whispered. 'I don't care what Mrs Medlock says, I'm going to find out.'

Candlestick in hand, she walked softly along the corridors. She saw a light shining under a door. She pushed the door open and there, lying on a four-poster bed, she saw a boy crying pitifully.

He turned suddenly and stopped crying. 'Are you a ghost?' he asked, frightened.

'No, I'm Mary Lennox,' she answered. 'Who are you?'

'I'm Mr Craven's son, Colin,' said the boy.

'So I must be your cousin,' Mary went on. 'Did no one tell you I'd come to live here?'

'No. No one would dare,' replied Colin. 'I should have been afraid you'd see me. My father won't let people see me. He's afraid I'll grow up to be a hunchback. I'm always ill and so I stay here in bed. My father hates me because my mother died when I was born.'

'Have you always been here?' asked Mary.

'Nearly always,' Colin answered. 'If I go out, people stare at me and I can't stand it.'

'If you don't like people to see you, shall I go away?' Mary asked.

'Oh, no!' Colin answered quickly. 'Stay and talk to me.'

They talked for a long time. Mary learned how miserable Colin felt. He was sure he would never get well.

'All the servants have to please me,' Colin told her. 'It makes me ill to be angry. Everyone has to do as I say.'

He asked Mary's age.

'I'm ten, the same as you,' she told him.

'How do you know I'm ten?' he asked.

'Because the garden was locked ten years ago when you were born,' Mary answered.

'What garden?' Colin asked.

'Just a garden Mr Craven hates,' Mary replied. 'He locked the door and buried the key.'

'What's the garden like?' Colin persisted.

'No one has been allowed to see it for ten years,' Mary answered. She was careful not to let him know she had already found it. They talked of all the exciting things that might be in the garden.

'I shall make them open the door,' Colin said.

'Oh, no!' cried Mary. 'Let's keep it a secret. If they open the door, it will never be a secret again. Perhaps one day we may find the door. We could go inside and no one would know about it but us.'

'I should like that,' said Colin. 'I never had a secret before.' Tired with talking, he fell asleep and Mary crept away.

The next morning, Mary told Martha about
the crying and how she had found Colin. Poor
Martha was very upset. She thought she
might lose her job for allowing Mary to find
the young master of the house.

'You needn't worry,' Mary told her. 'Colin
was pleased and he wants to see me every
day.'

'Tha must have bewitched him!' Martha
cried.

'What's the matter with him?' Mary asked.
Martha told her that since he was born, Colin
had not been allowed to walk. His father
thought his back was weak. A famous doctor
had been to see him, and said he would get
strong if less fuss was made of him.

'Colin thinks he will die,' said Mary. 'Do you think so?'

'Mother says there's no reason for a child to live if he can't get out in the fresh air,' Martha answered.

'It's done me good to be outside,' said Mary. 'Do you think it would help Colin?'

'Eh! I don't know,' Martha said. 'He had a bad tantrum when he was taken into the garden. He got angry because he thought one of the gardeners was looking at him. He cried so much he was ill all night.'

'Well,' said Mary, 'if he ever gets angry with me, I shan't go to see him again.'

On her next visit to Colin, Mary told him about Dickon.

'He's not like anyone else in the world,' she said. 'He can charm the animals on the moor. When he plays on his pipe, they come to listen.'

'The moor sounds a wonderful place,' said Colin, 'but I'll never see it. I'm going to die.'

'How do you know?' Mary asked, feeling a little cross. Colin talked about dying almost as though it pleased him.

'Everyone says I will,' Colin answered. 'I think my father will be glad when I'm not here.'

'I don't believe that,' said Mary. 'That famous doctor was right. They should make less fuss of you and they should let you go out. Oh! If you could see Dickon, you'd want to get well.' And she told him all about Dickon's family who were so well and happy even though they were so poor.

It rained for a week so Mary could not visit the garden. Instead, she spent her days with Colin. They read and talked and, for the first time, Colin started to laugh. Often he spoke of the garden and what might be in it. Mary longed to share her secret with him but felt that she could not yet trust him.

After the rain, Mary awoke early one morning to find the sun streaming through the blinds. When she ran down to the Secret Garden, she found that Dickon was already there.

'I couldn't stay in bed on a morning like this,' he cried. 'Look at th' garden!' The rain and the warmth had made all the new shoots push up through the earth. There were clumps of orange and purple crocuses. Mary was breathless with happiness. The robin was building a nest.

'We mustn't watch too close,' warned Dickon. 'He's too busy now for visitin' an' gossipin'.'

A whole week had passed since Mary had seen Dickon. She told him about finding Colin.

'If we could get him out here,' said Dickon, 'he'd forget about lumps growing on his back. We'd be just two lads and a little lass lookin' on at th' Springtime. I could push his chair. It'd do him more good than doctor's stuff.'

When Mary went in at the end of the day, Martha told her that Colin was angry because she had not been to see him.

'I won't let that boy come if you stay with him instead of me,' Colin raged when Mary saw him. 'You're selfish for not coming!'

'What are you?' snapped Mary. 'You're the most selfish person I know!'

'Well, I'm going to die!' wailed Colin.

'I don't believe it,' said Mary sourly. 'You only want people to be sorry for you. But they're not! You're too nasty!' She marched to the door and called back, 'I was going to tell you about Dickon and his fox and crow, but I shan't now.' And she shut the door firmly behind her.

In her room, she thought of Colin's lonely day. Her anger faded and she felt sorry for him. 'If he wants me tomorrow,' she thought, 'I'll go and see him.'

In the night, Mary was awakened by noises in the corridor and she could hear sobbing and screaming. 'It's Colin having a tantrum,' she thought. She covered her ears but couldn't shut out the dreadful sounds.

She jumped out of bed and stamped her foot angrily. 'Somebody must stop him,' she cried. 'He deserves beating for being so selfish! He's upsetting everyone in the house!' She ran into Colin's room and shouted, 'You stop! I hate you! You'll scream yourself to death in a minute and I wish you would!'

Colin looked dreadful. His face was swollen and he was gasping and choking but Mary was too angry to care. 'If you scream again, I shall scream louder!' she stormed.

'I can't stop,' sobbed Colin. 'I've felt a lump coming on my back.'

'Turn over and let me look,' snapped Mary. She looked carefully at the poor thin back. 'There's not a lump as big as a pin,' she announced. 'Don't you ever talk about it again!'

Colin's sobbing slowly died and Mary sat by his bed quietly comforting him until he fell asleep.

In the morning, Mary found Dickon in the garden with his squirrels, and she told him of Colin's sobbing in the night. 'Eh! We mun' get him out here, poor lad!' he said.

'Aye, that we mun',' said Mary, using the same Yorkshire words.

Dickon laughed. 'Tha mun' talk a bit o' Yorkshire to Colin,' he said. 'It'll make him laugh and Mother says laughing's good for ill folk.'

When Mary went in to Colin she told him the morning's news of Dickon and his squirrels, Nut and Shell. They laughed and talked for a long time.

Then Colin said, 'I'm sorry I said I'd send Dickon away. I didn't mean it. He's a wonderful boy.'

'I'm glad you said that,' said Mary, 'because he's coming to see you and he's bringing his animals.'

Colin cheered up. He looked so happy that suddenly Mary decided to take a chance and trust him. 'But that's not all,' she went on. 'There's something better! I've found the door to the garden!'

Colin was overjoyed. 'Then shall we go in and find out what's inside?' he asked.

Mary paused and then boldly told the truth. 'I've already been in it. That's why I could tell you so much about it. I daren't tell you my secret until I was sure I could trust you.'

At breakfast, Colin announced to his nurse, 'A boy and some animals are coming to see me. Bring them straight up when they arrive.'

It wasn't long before Mary heard a bleating. 'That's Dickon's lamb!' she cried. 'They're coming!'

Dickon came in smiling. He carried a lamb, and his little red fox trotted beside him. Nut, the squirrel, sat on one shoulder and the crow on the other. His other squirrel, Shell, peeped out of a pocket.

Colin stared in wonder. Dickon gently put the lamb in Colin's lap and gave him a bottle to feed it. They were all so busy and happy together. Dickon had endless tales to tell.

'I'm going to see it all!' cried Colin.

'Aye, that tha mun',' said Mary, 'an' tha munnot lose no time about it.'

Colin was put in his chair and Dickon pushed it along the paths. As they went, Mary told Colin about the places they passed. 'Here's where I met Ben,' she said, 'and this is where I saw the robin. And this,' she whispered, 'this is the garden!'

Mary opened the door and Dickon pushed the chair inside quickly. Colin looked round for a long time seeing all the things Mary had described. Then he cried out, 'I shall get well! I shall live for ever and ever!' That afternoon, the whole world changed for Colin.

'It's been a grand day,' said Dickon.

'Aye, that it has,' said Mary.

'Does tha think,' said Colin, 'that it was made like this 'ere all for me?'

'My word!' said Mary, 'That's a good bit of Yorkshire.' And they all joined in the laughter.

'I don't want this day to go,' said Colin, 'but I shall come back every day.'

'That tha will,' said Dickon, 'an' we shall soon have thee digging and walking.'

Suddenly, Ben Weatherstaff's face glared down at them from the top of the wall. 'What are you doing in there?' he shouted at Mary. Then he saw Colin and his mouth opened in surprise.

'Do you know who I am?' Colin asked.

'Aye, that I do,' Ben answered. 'Th'art th' poor cripple lad.'

Colin sat up angrily. 'I'm not a cripple! I'll show you!' he cried. With Dickon's help, he struggled out of the chair and stood, straight and tall. 'Look at me now!' he shouted.

'God bless thee, lad!' smiled Ben and tears ran down his face.

Colin remained standing. He suddenly felt his fear leave him. 'I'm not afraid any more!' he cried. 'It's the magic of the Secret Garden! It's working to make all the plants grow and it will work for me.'

That evening Colin was quiet. At last, he said to Mary, 'I'm not going to be a poor thing any more. If I believe I shall get strong and well, the magic will make it happen.'

Next day in the garden, Colin called Mary, Dickon and Ben to him. 'I'm going to show you that the magic works,' he said.

Slowly, taking a few steps at a time, Colin walked right round the garden. His face was flushed with joy.

'This must be the biggest secret of all,' he said. 'When I can walk and run well, I shall walk into my father's study and I'll say, ''Here I am, well and strong!'''

It was very hard to keep the secret. The magic of the Secret Garden was making Colin bright-eyed and rosy-cheeked. Each day Colin and Mary did exercises to make them strong and they both grew plumper and healthier. Mary lost her sour, ugly look and became pretty. Colin no longer looked like an invalid. Everyone was amazed at the change.

One morning Colin stopped digging. He suddenly felt different. 'Look at me!' he cried. 'I'm well! I'm really well! I want to shout for joy! I shall live for ever and ever!'

Now while the Secret Garden was working its magic, Mr Craven was travelling in faraway places. For ten years he had tried to run away from his sorrow and had refused to be comforted.

One day, whilst walking in Austria, he sat down by a stream. Gradually, he felt his mind and body grow quiet. The peace of the place filled him and from that moment he felt healthier and happier.

One night, he dreamt of his wife's garden at Misselthwaite Manor. The dream was so clear he decided he must return home at once. As soon as he arrived home, he went into the garden.

His steps were slow. All the sad memories of his lovely wife came back to him. As he stood outside the door of the Secret Garden, wondering how to find the key, he heard the sound of laughter from inside.

Suddenly, the door burst open and a boy ran out, almost into his arms. He was a tall, handsome boy and Mr Craven gazed at him, unable to speak.

Colin stood still and recovered his breath. Then he said, 'Father, I'm Colin. You can't believe it but it's true.'

He led his father into the garden and told him how the magic had made everything grow and had made him strong and well.

Mr Craven had never heard such a wonderful story. He sat by Mary and Dickon and the animals and listened and laughed as he had not done for years. He was so proud of his handsome, healthy son!

'Now,' said Colin at the end of the story, 'it needn't be a secret any more. I shall never need my chair again. I shall walk with you, Father!'

They stood up, and Mr Craven walked across the lawn to the house. At his side, strong and straight as any lad in Yorkshire, walked his son.

Stories . . . that have stood the test of time

SERIES 740
FABLES
Aladdin and his wonderful lamp
Ali Baba and the forty thieves
Famous Legends (Book 1)
Famous Legends (Book 2)
A first book of Aesop's Fables
A second book of Aesop's Fables
La Fontaine's Fables:
The Fox turned Wolf
Folk Tales from around the World

LADYBIRD CHILDREN'S CLASSICS
Treasure Island
Swiss Family Robinson
Secret Garden
A Journey to the Centre of the Earth
The Three Musketeers
A Tale of Two Cities
Gulliver's Travels
The Lost World

Ladybird titles cover a wide range of subjects and reading ages.
Write for a free illustrated list from the publishers:
LADYBIRD BOOKS LTD Loughborough Leicestershire England